LION HOUSE, LINCOLN PARK ZOO

CHICAGO, ILLINOIS

UNiVERSiTY MUSEUM of
ARCHAEOLOGY AND ANTHROPOLOGY,
UNiVERSiTY OF PENNSYLVANiA

PHiLADELPHiA, PENNSYLVANiA

IMMIGRANT ARCHITECT

This is me standing beside my father
on the day we arrived in New York.

CITY HALL

IMMIGRANT ARCHITECT
~RAFAEL GUASTAVINO AND THE AMERICAN DREAM~

Written by Berta de Miguel, Kent Diebolt, and Virginia Lorente • Illustrated by Virginia Lorente

TILBURY HOUSE PUBLISHERS, THOMASTON, MAINE

R. GUASTAVINO

DEDICATIONS

To all immigrants, especially my three favorites: Gala, Marlo, and Gabi.
I wish you a life without borders, forever full of curiosity. —B.M.

To migrants everywhere who have risked everything for a better future, and to past,
present, and future generations of Guastavino boys and girls, including George Collins,
Bob Silman, Janet Parks, Derek Trelstad, John Ochsendorf, Fernando Vegas, Camilla
Mileto, Jose Luis Gonzalez, Gloria Riba Francas, and my co-authors! —K.D.

To Eva and Marina. Never give up on your dreams. —V.L.

- -

Library of Congress Control Number: 2019957057 • Book design by Frame25 Productions

Printed in China through Four Colour Print Group • 18 19 20 XXX 10 9 8 7 6 5 4 3 2 1

Tilbury House Publishers • Thomaston, Maine • www.tilburyhouse.com

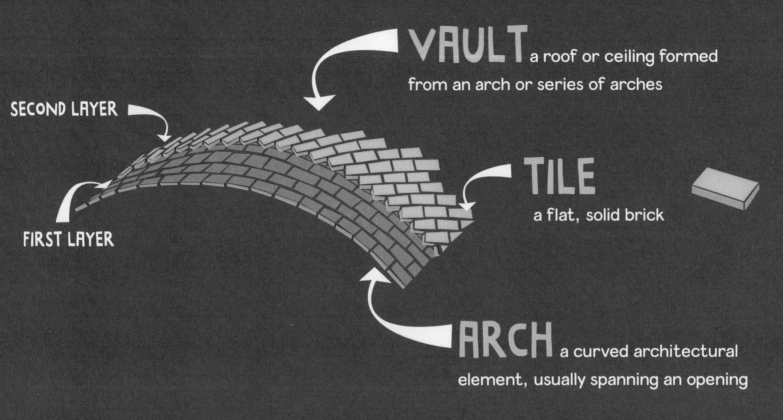

VAULT a roof or ceiling formed from an arch or series of arches

SECOND LAYER

FIRST LAYER

TILE a flat, solid brick

ARCH a curved architectural element, usually spanning an opening

DOME a rounded vault, typically with a circular base

THIS IS
THE STORY
ABOUT A

BIG

THE
STORY
ABOUT

DREAM

GUASTAVINO

Actually it is a story about **two** people named Guastavino.

Rafael Guastavino Moreno was a visionary, an architect, an engineer, an artist, an interior designer, an immigrant to America, a musician . . . and **my father**.

R. GUASTAVINO

I too am named Rafael, like my father and grandfather. I am Rafael III. My full name is Rafael Guastavino Expósito, and I would like to tell you how my father and I emigrated from Spain and changed the shape and color of a thousand buildings in the **United States**.

My father was born in **Valencia**, Spain, in 1842.

The City of Valencia has many domes in its skyline and also has a very special light because it is close to the Mediterranean Sea.

My father grew up in a house in the city center, a neighborhood with majestic historic buildings constructed with fantastic vaulted ceilings.

My great great grandfather was a leading architect and my grandfather was a piano builder and restorer. My father wanted to become both a violinist and an architect.

It is good to have dreams!

1842
▼

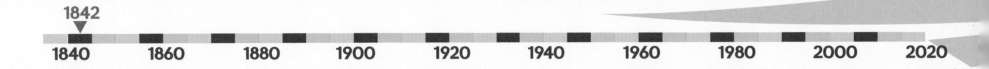

1840   1860   1880   1900   1920   1940   1960   1980   2000   2020

At the age of seventeen, my father moved to **Barcelona**, where he learned how to design and construct wonderful buildings.

After he became a master builder, he designed a number of homes and industrial buildings in and around Barcelona that were inspirations for future famous architects.

He incorporated vaulted and domed ceilings into many of his earliest designs.

La Massa theater was one of the most famous buildings he designed. He gave this building an extraordinary large and very thin **domed ceiling** constructed of tiles.

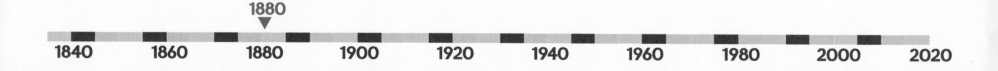

1880

1840 1860 1880 1900 1920 1940 1960 1980 2000 2020

LA MASSA THEATER, VILASSAR DE DALT, CATALONIA, SPAIN

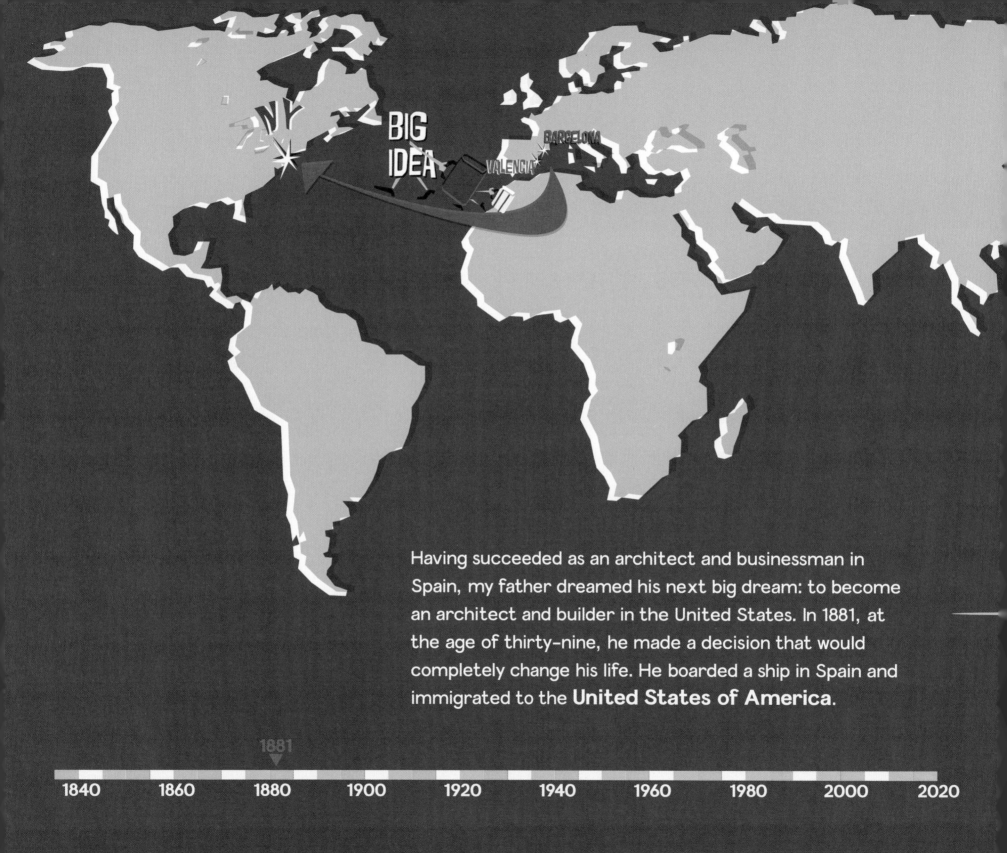

Having succeeded as an architect and businessman in Spain, my father dreamed his next big dream: to become an architect and builder in the United States. In 1881, at the age of thirty-nine, he made a decision that would completely change his life. He boarded a ship in Spain and immigrated to the **United States of America**.

1881

| 1840 | 1860 | 1880 | 1900 | 1920 | 1940 | 1960 | 1980 | 2000 | 2020 |

He brought two things with him: a **BIG** idea and . . . **ME!** He wasn't just changing his own life; he was changing mine, too. I was only eight years old and not at all sure what our future held.

Although I was thrilled with the adventure, saying goodbye to my siblings and especially to my **mamá** was very difficult. As often happens with emigrant families, I didn't know if I would ever see her again.

It was a **long trip** by ship. It took us two weeks to travel from Barcelona to New York City.

The United States was a young, growing, exciting country in the midst of what is now called its **Gilded Age**. Railroads were expanding, new territories were being developed and settled, and commerce and trade were exploding.

For instance, can you imagine a city that grows from 1 million to 3.5 million inhabitants in twenty years? That is what happened to **New York City** in the two decades after we arrived.

When we arrived, the Brooklyn Bridge was still under construction but was almost finished.

New York, Boston, and other cities across the United States needed new houses, bridges, tunnels, schools, universities, churches, public baths (because at that time there were no showers at home), gyms, banks, hospitals, museums . . . They needed everything!

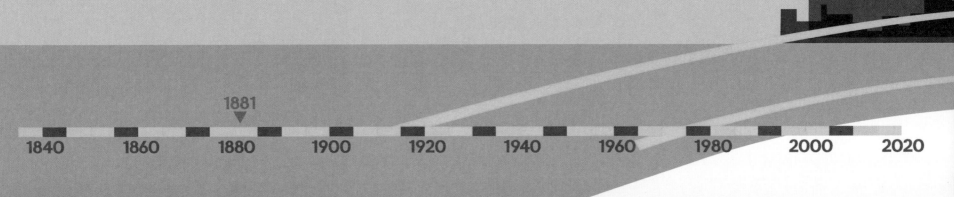

1881

1840   1860   1880   1900   1920   1940   1960   1980   2000   2020

It was a perfect environment for
an **architect**, don't you think?

The country also needed thousands of immigrants to help make all this growth possible.

When immigrants arrive in a new country, they are drawn to people from their own culture, who speak their native language and share their customs. That is the origin of ethnic **neighborhoods** such as Little Italy, Chinatown, and others. We also followed this path and went to live in Little Spain, a neighborhood on the west side of Manhattan around 14th Street. My father and I didn't speak any English, which made everything difficult.

My father decided to send me to a boarding school to learn English; at first I was terrified of being all by myself, but I soon made new friends. I graduated with honors **one year later** and went back to New York to start helping my dad in his office.

Imagine! I was only ten years old and spoke better English than he did.

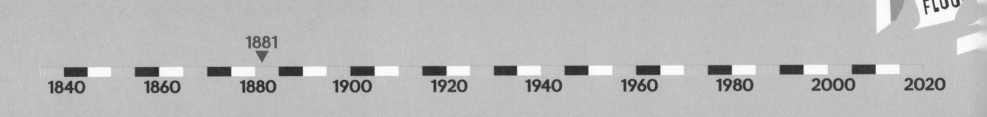

1881

1840   1860   1880   1900   1920   1940   1960   1980   2000   2020

While I was away at school, my father tried hard to find work as an architect, but because he spoke so little English, he made little progress.

In the 1880s, American cities had a problem. A huge problem. Buildings were often constructed mainly of wood or iron, and both materials behave terribly in the presence of **fire**: wood burns into ashes, and iron deforms and melts. In either case, the building collapses and the result is disastrous.

Buildings were also constructed very close together. When one ignited, the fire could spread across the block and through the neighborhood in a matter of minutes.

Fires were common in America's growing cities. In 1871, the Great Fire of Chicago destroyed the houses of 100,000 inhabitants. Seventy-three miles of roads, 2,000 lampposts, and 17,500 buildings were lost.

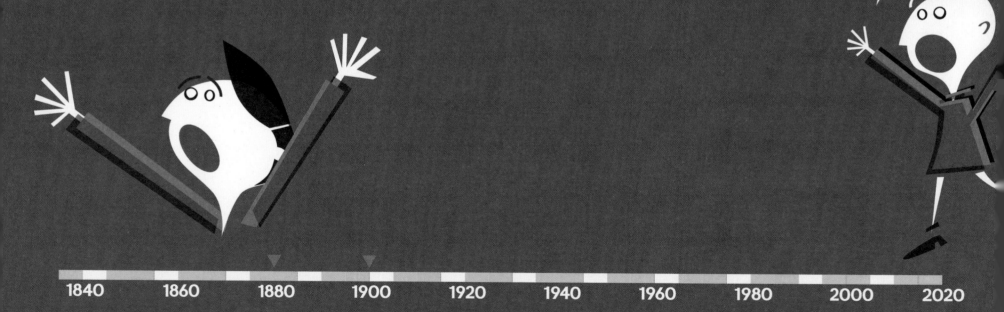

| 1840 | 1860 | 1880 | 1900 | 1920 | 1940 | 1960 | 1980 | 2000 | 2020 |

American citizens were understandably **very afraid of fires**, especially in densely packed cities!

My father had come to America with a unique **solution** to this problem.

Do you know what high-temperature pizza and bread ovens are made of? **BRICKS!**
That is because bricks can withstand extremely high temperatures.

My father knew how to enclose interior spaces with complex curved surfaces
constructed from very thin bricks—called ceramic tiles—and how to make the spaces
fireproof by building what architects call vaults, which are arched roofs and ceilings.

Isn't that brilliant? Real brilliance is often hidden in the simplest
ideas, the ones that seem so obvious you wonder why no
one has thought of them before.

That is the **big idea** that my father had carried
aboard the ship from Spain! It had given him the
confidence to emigrate.

1840   1860   1880   1900   1920   1940   1960   1980   2000   2020

My father patented tiled vaults and domes as a fireproof construction system after we arrived in America, so he was the only one who could legally use the system in the United States. That is how this construction type became known as the **Guastavino tile vaulting system**. His system made buildings strong, fireproof, and beautiful.

Layers of interlocking flat tiles and mortar can form a thin yet strong shell that can be curved almost any way you can imagine. A vault built like this is like an eggshell, light but strong thanks to its overall shape.

Try this experiment:

Squeeze an egg endwise between your thumb and forefinger, and you will be surprised how strong it is. You may not be able to break it! Its strength is due to its shape. Vaults, arches, and domes work the same way.

Now squeeze an egg the other way and see what happens!

Nobody in the United States had heard of tile vaults. To promote the fireproof and structural properties of a tile vault and to convince the building-code authorities of the safety of the system, my father set up demonstrations in which he built a fire under a vault and weighed it down with tons of iron weights—**up to 120,000 pounds!!!**

Do you know how much weight that is? It's like stacking **eight large elephants** on top of a vault!

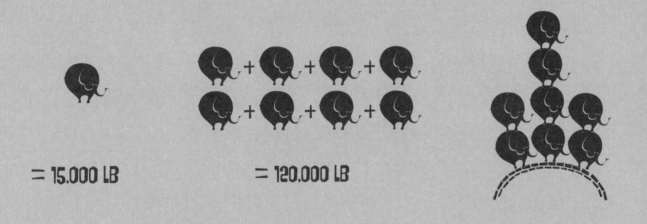

= 15,000 LB   = 120,000 LB

A lot of people—including architects, officials, engineers, building owners, and the press—attended these demonstrations.

1840   1860   1880   1900   1920   1940   1960   1980   2000   2020

They were all astonished by what they witnessed.

They wondered how a Guastavino vault could possibly resist hours of fire and tons of weight without falling apart.

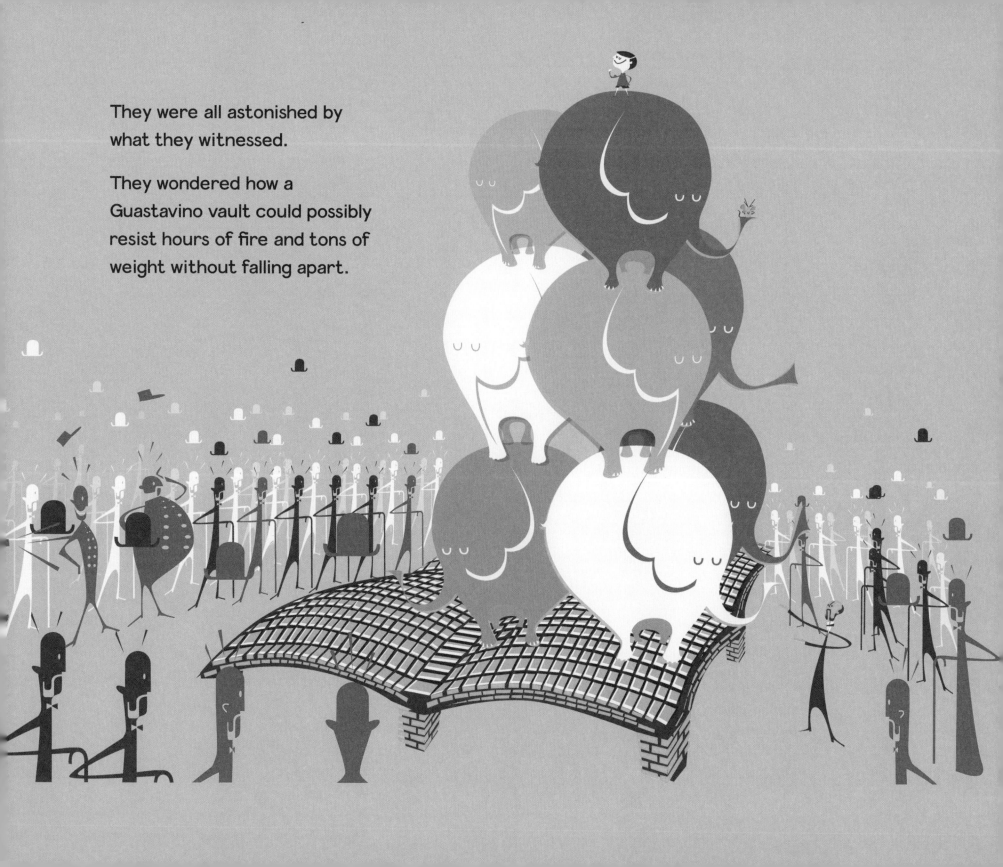

And yet, despite all the recommendations and achievements my father had brought with him from Spain, and despite all his demonstrations and explanations, he could not find projects to design. Builders and other architects had a hard time understanding his terrible English.

To earn money, he took a job as an illustrator for a furniture magazine. He was an exceptional illustrator and could draw anything. Drawing is an international language through which he was more than capable of communicating. Eventually, his illustrations led to architectural design work, which led to his first big commission as a building contractor, the Boston Public Library, which led to the formation of **the Guastavino Fireproof Construction Company**.

Remember, I was ten years old when I started working for my father's company parttime after school. At the age of fifteen I began working there fulltime.

1840   1860   1880   1900   1920   1940   1960   1980   2000   2020

My father designed the ceilings of the Boston Public Library in 1889, working with the superstar architects of the time, McKim, Mead & White.

The library's ceilings served as a Guastavino company catalog. They were constructed in a variety of **patterns** with a variety of decorative details.

The Boston Public Library was the first library in the United States to lend books for free to any citizen. That is why it was known as the **Palace for the People**.

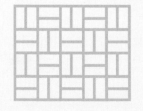 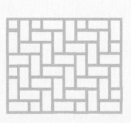   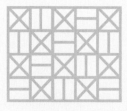 

1889

1840   1860   1880   1900   1920   1940   1960   1980   2000   2020

BOSTON PUBLIC LIBRARY

In the beginning, we risked everything to win new projects and overcome challenges. Sometimes we were successful, and sometimes we lost everything.

Once we lost our house and had to sleep in our office, pretending to work late so that nobody knew we were living there. I remember when my father sold his beloved violin to our landlady in order to pay the rent.

My father was one of the bravest and most determined people I have ever known. **He never gave up.** The poorer and more desperate we might be, the more creative, excited, and focused he became to solve our problems.

That is something we ALL should keep in mind. If you fail, take it as **an opportunity to learn, move forward, and succeed.**

1894

| 1840 | 1860 | 1880 | 1900 | 1920 | 1940 | 1960 | 1980 | 2000 | 2020 |

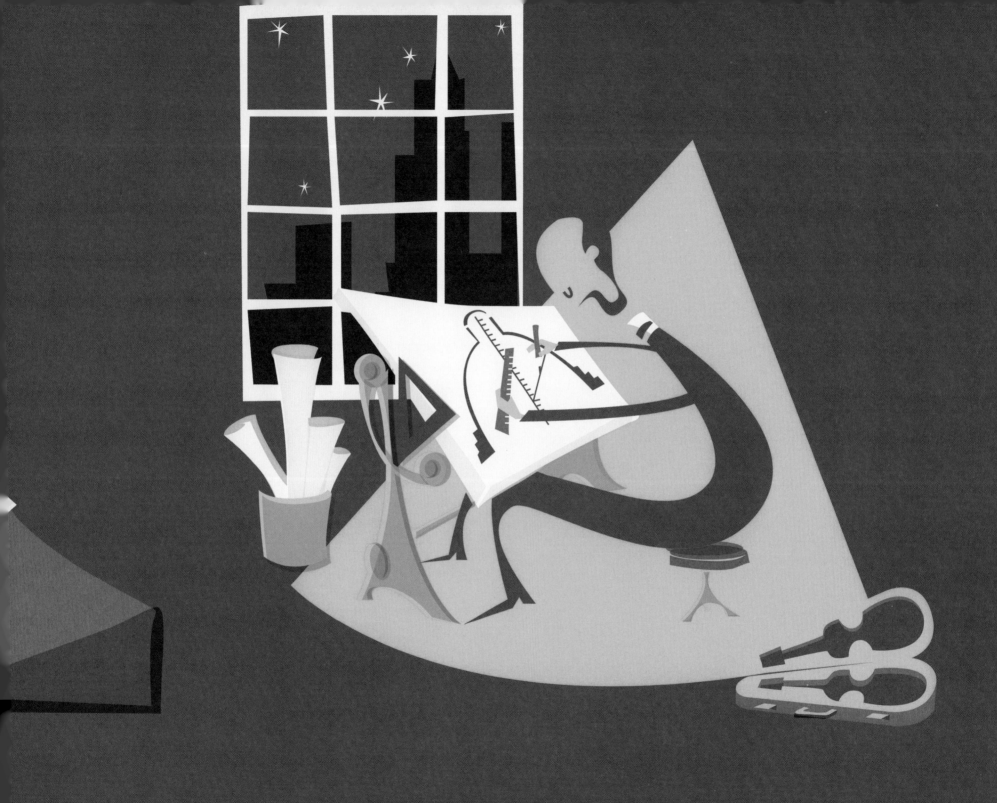

And
that is how we got one of
our most successful projects, the
first subway station in the City of New York.

When the subway system was constructed, New Yorkers were
worried about traveling underground because they were afraid
the ceilings might collapse. To ease their fears, my father designed the
station with bright colors, luxurious lighting, and even skylights. It looked
more like a palace dining room than an underground subway station. Thanks
in part to his work, New Yorkers became unafraid of traveling on subways.

SECRET: The train station was closed and abandoned in 1945 because trains
got longer. Now it is probably the most beautiful ghost space in the city, and
the best part is that you can see it. If you take the Number 6 train downtown
and stay in it after the last stop, it makes a U-turn through the Guastavino
station before heading back uptown. Press your forehead to the glass and you
will see sunlight streaming in through the skylights to illuminate my father's
ghost station. **What an imaginative and magical space!**

1904
▼

1840 1860 1880 1900 1920 1940 1960 1980 2000 2020

CITY HALL SUBWAY

In the late 1890s my father went to live in the Black Mountains near Asheville, North Carolina, where he was working on the 250-room Biltmore House, the largest home in America. With his help, I began directing the company in New York.

I was just twenty-two years old, but my father had taught me enough that I could begin running the Guastavino Fireproof Construction Company on my own.

In 1906 my father designed and started building the St. Lawrence Basilica in Asheville with an unusual and fabulous oval dome. During the winter of 1908, he caught a cold while working on the cathedral site and died unexpectedly in February, just after the main dome was completed.

His funeral service was held in the unfinished church, accompanied by music of his own composition. Sadly, he never had a chance to return to Spain and never saw his family again.

I was devastated by the sudden death of the father who had inspired me, but life had to continue. I took over management of the company, and my father's dream become mine: to help build the new world.

1908

1840   1860   1880   1900   1920   1940   1960   1980   2000   2020

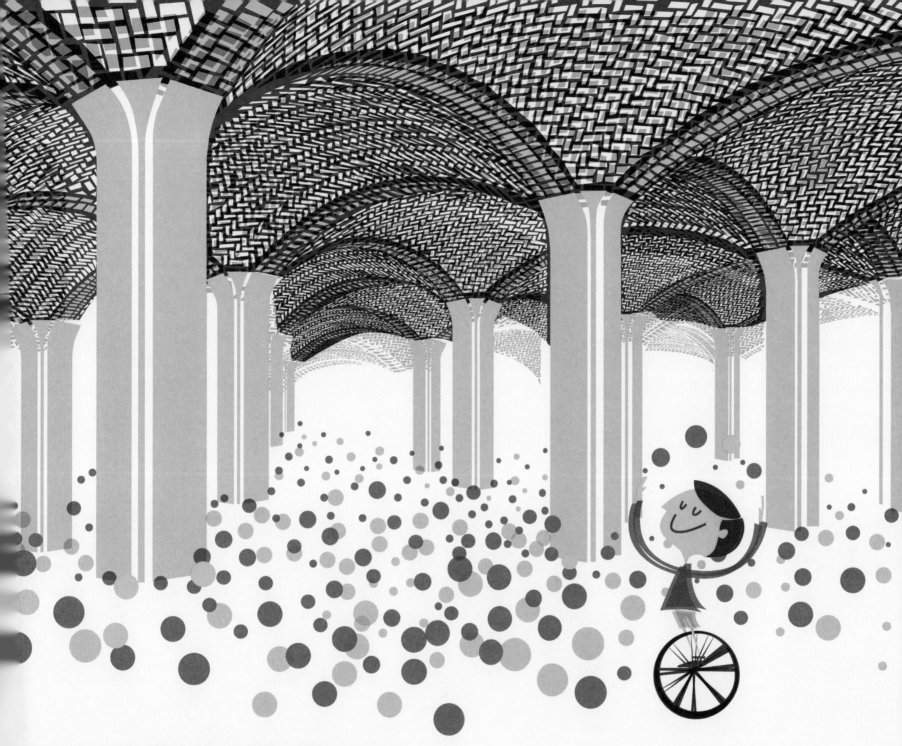

know that the **New York City Marathon**
into Manhattan over this bridge?

QUEENSBORO BRIDGE

One of my favorite projects was the elephant house at the Bronx Zoo, which, by the way, was one of the first **zoos** in the world.

This is where the elephants sleep and take refuge from the rain, and it is **gorgeous!**

The dome has **skylights** that allow natural light to enter the space. The effect is similar to that of dappled sunlight filtered through a forest canopy, so the elephants feel at home.

ELEPHANT HOUSE

You may be wondering what is the biggest dome we ever erected. It is the central dome of the Cathedral Church of St. John the Divine in New York City.

This dome is 95 feet in diameter, and its thickness varies from 8 inches at the base to just 3.5 inches at the top. It is so tall—162 feet—that the Statue of Liberty could stand beneath it, yet it was built in just **three months**! My father would have been so proud.

In this cathedral are two Guastavino staircases whose main feature is that they lack a central axis. Each staircase seems to be floating in the air.

SECRET: Many people don't know that this dome was intended to remain only until the cathedral raised enough funds to replace it with a central tower. But this **never happened**.

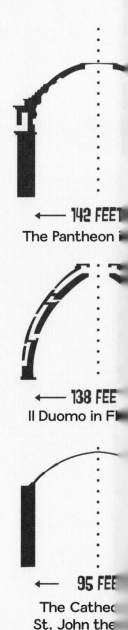

← 142 FEET
The Pantheon i

← 138 FEE
Il Duomo in Fl

← 95 FEE
The Cathed
St. John the

1909
▼

1840 1860 1880 1900 1920 1940 1960 1980 2000

ST. JOHN THE DIVINE DOME

New
York City used to
have two fantastic main train stations,
Grand Central Terminal and Pennsylvania Station,
which was said to be the most beautiful station in the
world. Both stations featured Guastavino vaults.

Unfortunately, and despite intense opposition, the original Penn Station was demolished in 1964 to be replaced by a more modern train station and related development projects. When plans were announced to tear down and replace Grand Central Terminal as well, outraged New Yorkers created an activist movement that saved it. Today Grand Central Terminal remains one of the most cherished public spaces in America. More than 750,000 people pass through this station every day.

SECRET: In the basement of Grand Central, at the entrance to the Oyster Bar Restaurant, you will find one of the most famous Guastavino vaults. It does not look special, but it is called **the whispering gallery**. Can you imagine why?

1912
▼

1840   1860   1880   1900   1920   1940   1960   1980   2000

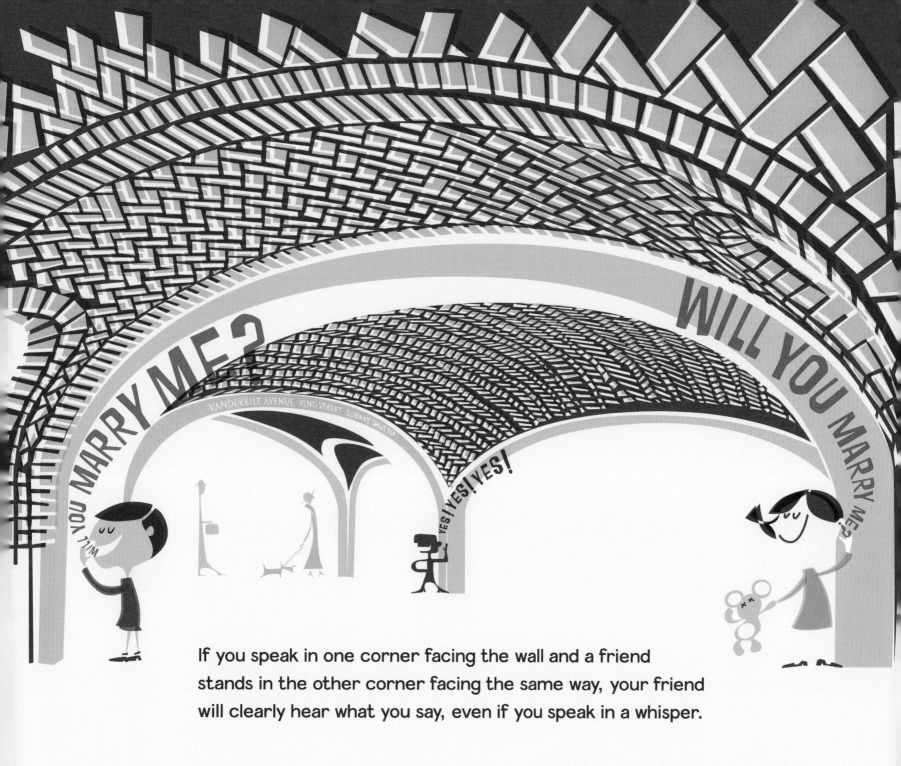

If you speak in one corner facing the wall and a friend stands in the other corner facing the same way, your friend will clearly hear what you say, even if you speak in a whisper.

GRAND CENTRAL TERMINAL

In 1912 we finished the most fashionable and luxurious hotel of its
day in New York, the Vanderbilt Hotel.

The most fabulous space was the lobby and bar at ground level, which featured spectacular
Guastavino vaulted ceilings with **polychromatic** (multicolored) tiles.

Unfortunately, because New York is such a restless, constantly changing city, it too was
demolished in 1967. But a corner of the hotel was saved, and today, that corner is the
vaulted ceiling of Wolfgang's Steakhouse.

It is so dramatic that customers are distracted, **looking up** to admire the ceiling
vaults rather than paying attention to their meals.

1912
▼

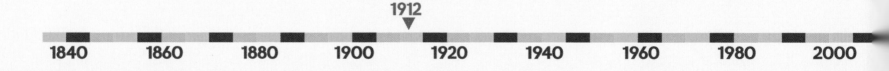

1840   1860   1880   1900   1920   1940   1960   1980   2000

DERBILT HOTEL

From the 1890s to the 1920s, millions of immigrants voyaged to the United States. Every single day, several ships would dock in New York City with hundreds of people carrying hundreds of dreams. **Ellis Island** was the largest immigration entry station in America. The more than 12 million immigrants who passed through its doors between 1892 and its closing in 1954 were not only welcomed, they were needed—just as they are needed today.

I was asked to design and build the vault that would cover the main hall, which was the first space millions of immigrants would see in America. Because I was an immigrant myself, this was a special project for me. I wanted them to feel **welcomed by their new country**.

FACT: Many of the grandparents of people you know came to America through Ellis Island. It is estimated that more than 40 percent of Americans today are descended from Ellis Island immigrants.

1917

1840   1860   1880   1900   1920   1940   1960   1980   2000

I have thought a lot about which building I would like to show you as this story comes to an end.

I have decided to finish with the color explosion of the **Nebraska State Capitol domes**. These ceilings were designed to tell stories about life, nature, society, agriculture, and native plants and animals.

The Nebraska State Capitol is so large and complicated that it took us ten years to complete the project!

Along with the featured polychromatic tiles, we also used tiles with special acoustic properties to soften the soundwaves echoing between the walls. This makes conversations in these spaces more understandable and pleasant.

I have always felt that this building represented the height of our achievement as a company. We combined shape, color, and sound control using curved tiled ceilings that are also structural.

1931

| 1840 | 1860 | 1880 | 1900 | 1920 | 1940 | 1960 | 1980 | 2000 |

COURAGE WISDOM

NEBRASKA STATE CAPITOL

The Guastavino Fireproof Construction Company, directed first by my father and then by me, built curved ceilings in more than one thousand buildings in ten countries, including Canada, Cuba, Holland, India, Mexico, Panama, Spain, Trinidad, and England as well as the US. In New York City alone, we helped design and construct vaults in more than 400 buildings.

When we arrived in America as immigrants from Spain, we brought and adapted a construction technique that would protect millions of lives from fire and would change the color and shapes of ceilings all over the United States.

Many architects and engineers were and still are inspired by the Guastavino vault: Antoni Gaudí, Lluis Domènech, Rosario Candela, Eladio Dieste, Fernando Vegas, Camilla Mileto, Norman Foster . . . .

And me? I forgot to tell you that I died in 1950. My words reach you now as if carried around the vaulted walls of the whispering gallery in Grand Central Terminal. Books, too, are vaults. They keep the past alive.

Know this:

You are our future. And knowing and protecting the past will help you create that future.

1840   1860   1880   1900   1920   1940   1960   1980   2000

Although some of our architecture has been demolished, there are still hundreds of buildings constructed with Guastavino tile that you can visit. Here are four suggested routes in New York City, and there are many others in other cities and countries.

UPTOWN ROUTE

Bronx Zoo Elephant House >The Cathedral Church of St. John the Divine

MIDTOWN ROUTE

Queensboro Bridge > Saint Thomas Church Fifth Avenue > St Bartholomew's Church > Grand Central Terminal > Wolfgang's Steakhouse (Park Avenue)

DOWNTOWN ROUTE

Municipal building subway entrance > Western Union Building (60 Hudson Street) > 40 West St. Barclay–Vesey Building > National Museum of the American Indian > Battery Maritime Building

PROSPECT PARK ROUTE

Prospect Park Zoo Entrance Shelter > Tennis Shelter > Prospect Park Boathouse + Audubon Center > The Peristyle, Croquet Shelter

1840 1860 1880 1900 1920 1940 1960 1980 2000

UPTOWN
ROUTE

MIDTOWN
ROUTE

DOWNTOWN
ROUTE

PROSPECT PARK
ROUTE

DOWNTOWN
ROUTE

RAFAEL GUASTAVINO MORENO

Born: Valencia, Spain, 1842 • **Died:** Baltimore, 1908

Adventurous architect and visionary, he emigrated with his son, Rafael Guastavino Expósito, to the USA in 1881. He improved and patented the tiled vault as a fireproof construction technique with which he designed amazing curved architecture, changing the shape and color of ceilings in the United States.

R. GUASTAVINO

RAFAEL GUASTAVINO EXPÓSITO

Born: Barcelona, Spain, 1873 • **Died:** New York, 1950

Fearless son, he was only eight years old when he embarked on a journey with his faher that would change his life forever. Fascinated by the amazing curved architecture that his father imported to the USA, he continued the work of the Guastavino Company and designed the most beautiful, colorful, enormous vaults that can ever be seen.

ACKNOWLEDGMENTS

In 1965, an architecture professor named **George Collins** was studying the history of Spanish architecture at Columbia University. One day he looked up at the ceiling and saw an extraordinary Guastavino dome. Realizing that he had no knowledge of the dome or the architect who designed it, he started investigating.

Our company had closed by then, but Collins went to our abandoned factory outside Boston and found, in the dumpster, hundreds of Guastavino Company architectural drawings. He recovered them and took his collection to the Avery Library at Columbia University.

Today that collection is called the **Guastavino–Collins archive**, and anyone can visit to study our original drawings.

Thank you, George Collins. Without you, our legacy might have been **forgotten**.

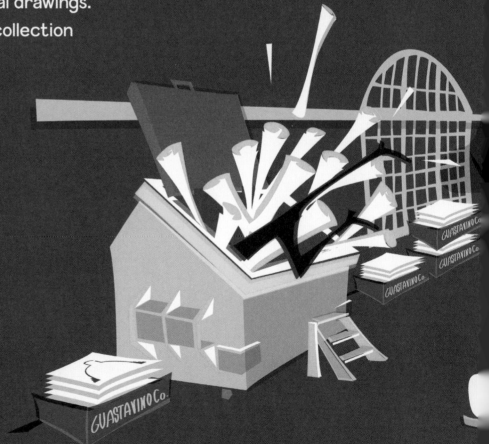

HEARST MEMORIAL MINING BUILDING VESTIBULE,
UNIVERSITY OF CALIFORNIA

BERKELEY, CALIFORNIA

UNITED STATES NATIONAL MUSEUM

WASHINGTON, D.C.

The Queensboro Bridge project was one of the first I managed on my own.

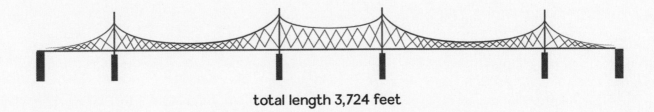

total length 3,724 feet

Soaring spaces under the Manhattan approach to the bridge are constructed of fantastic white-tiled Guastavino vaults. The space beneath the vaults became an open street market, and people liked it so much that the market became famous for sumptuous delicatessen foods.

When you look up at the ceiling vaults, you feel inspired by curves that look like a forest. The columns are tree trunks, and the curved vaults look like branched forest canopies.

An urban forest!

1908
▼

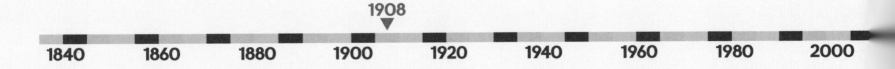

1840   1860   1880   1900   1920   1940   1960   1980   2000

BASILICA OF ST. LAWRENCE